Believathon II:
Journey to the Stronghold

THE COMPENDIUM

Table of Contents

Foreward   iii
Believathon II Map   iv-v
The Quester's Pledge   1
Believathon II Information   2
Important Dates   3
Believathon II Quest   4-17
The Prompts   18-21
Recommendations   22-44
The Magic of Middle Grade   45-52

Foreward

I constantly see how people are surprised by middle grade when they read it for the first time as an adult – most of the comments I get are along the lines of 'I can't believe how much I enjoyed it, I didn't think I would.' It's the best feeling in the world to see people give middle grade a chance, especially after we think we've grown out of it. But let's not underestimate middle grade. We may have grown out of the category, but our imaginations must never be limited by age. We must never give up on a story just because it's aimed for children – we could be missing out on a world that could teach us so much. There are lessons to be learned even as grown-ups, and I firmly believe that the older we get, the more we need to remember that magic truly exists between the pages of middle grade.

– Gavin

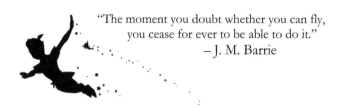

"The moment you doubt whether you can fly,
you cease for ever to be able to do it."

– J. M. Barrie

THE QUESTER'S PLEDGE

I, the seeker of adventure,
do solemnly swear on the
Noble Art of Magic,
that I will abide by the laws
of the land,
and that I will always
be truthful and wary
upon my quest,
and that I do not use
my magic for personal gain,
but to advance peace
and prosperity to the
inhabitants of the
Land of Make-Believathon.

Signed:

_____

Believathon II Information

Believathon II: Journey to the Stronghold is a two-week readathon dedicated to reading children's literature. The readathon will begin on May 11th and will end on May 24th, 2020.

Begin your adventure at the Poacher's Pocket Inn and follow the story to the end of your quest. There will be three different paths to choose from and your reading list will be dictated by the reading prompt at each location. Your journey will begin when you complete your first reading prompt at the Poacher's Pocket Inn.

In order to complete your quest, you must visit five locations – including the Poacher's Pocket Inn – and complete five reading prompts. However, if you do not wish to read five books in two weeks, then fear not! A mysterious stranger will provide you with a magic lamp upon completing the prompt at your starting location. You have three wishes to choose from, but you can only choose one wish to help you on your journey! You will discover what the wishes are later…

Believathon II: Journey to the Stronghold will be hosted on YouTube by **How to Train Your Gavin** and on the dedicated Twitter and Instagram pages for Believathon (**@Believathon**). Follow for more information.

Important Dates

When traversing the Land of Make-Believathon, it will be easy to lose track of time. We hope a helpful calendar will help you remember important events that will be happening over your two-week adventure.

May 11 – Your journey begins at the Poacher's Pocket Inn. There will be reading sprints all day (and for the next two weeks) on @Believathon. Use the hashtag #Believathon throughout the two weeks of participating.

May 16-17 – Weekend of Magic. Immerse yourself in your childhood favourites by re-watching the movies you grew up on and re-reading the books that shaped you.

May 20 – Show the Love. Use this day to spread positivity! If you've loved what you've read so far, use the hashtag #Believathon, tag the authors of the books you loved and tell them how much you loved it!

May 24 – Your journey ends at the Book-Keeper's Stronghold. Believathon II is over. Join me for a live show on How to Train Your Gavin to discuss your adventures.

Turn the page to begin
your adventure…

The Poacher's Pocket Inn

As you enjoy a pint of speckled pig at the Poacher's Pocket Inn, you notice a shift in the atmosphere. The clouds darken outside. You look outside the window to see a dark figure approaching the inn. He spots you through the window and makes haste to the door.

The wind howls as he opens the door and marches directly to your table. You lower the pint of speckled pig as he lowers himself in the seat opposite you. He knows your name…

Before you have a chance to reply, he begins to recount your incredible adventures the November before – he has heard all about your incredible skills traversing the Land of Make-Believathon. Now he needs your help…

An evil witch has placed a curse on the Book-Keeper Stronghold in the far North. Because of this curse, books have become trapped to everyone but you, so people in the Land of Make-Believathon are beginning to lose their imaginations. You are the only person with the courage and strength to embark on this quest.

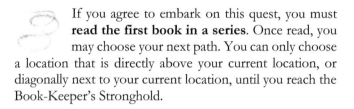 If you agree to embark on this quest, you must **read the first book in a series**. Once read, you may choose your next path. You can only choose a location that is directly above your current location, or diagonally next to your current location, until you reach the Book-Keeper's Stronghold.

But before you set off, the stranger thanks you with a magic lamp. The lamp can grant three wishes at any point in your journey, but you can only **choose one**:

1. Skip one location on your path.
2. Transport to a different next location on the map.
3. Transport to the Book-Keepers stronghold.

You're ready for your adventure, and now you must pick your next location, and stick to the path set before you unless you use one wish from the magic lamp. Be sure to choose your wish wisely.

Which location do you want to travel to?

The Yellow Brick Road – turn to page 6.
Baba Yaga's House – turn to page 7.
The Wonderfalls – turn to page 8.

The Book-Keeper's Stronghold – turn to page 15.

The Yellow Brick Road

As you're following the yellow brick road, you come across the Wicked Witch of the West! She enchants poppies around the path and causes you to fall into a deep slumber, one you fear you may never wake from.

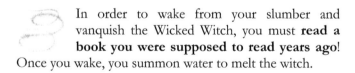

In order to wake from your slumber and vanquish the Wicked Witch, you must **read a book you were supposed to read years ago**! Once you wake, you summon water to melt the witch.

Which location do you want to travel to next?

100 Acre Wood – turn to page 9.

The Deepwoods – turn to page 10.

O n your path, you hear voices and music. You follow the sounds until you reach a fence with skills atop it, and just beyond lies a house! You approach but it stands – it's a house with chicken legs.

In order to enter, you must **read a book featuring a family relationship**! Once completed, Baba Yaga invites you inside. She prepares you *kvass* before sending you on your way!

Which location do you want to travel to next?

100 Acre Wood – turn to page 9.
The Deepwoods – turn to page 10.
Mermaids' Lagoon – turn to page 11.

The Wonderfalls

Everything is turning dark as you hear running water. As you get closer, you release it's not the trees blocking the sun – you've lost your sight! A warlock protecting the Wonderfalls has cursed you.

In order to regain your sight, you must **read a book featuring a disability**! Once completed, you use your other senses to vanquish the warlock and continue your journey through the Wonderfalls.

Which location do you want to travel to next?

The Deepwoods – turn to page 10.

Mermaids' Lagoon – turn to page 11.

A s you're walking, you come across a battered book that has been abandoned in the middle of the path. Wary, you approach, only to be pulled inside where you find yourself in the 100 Acre Wood. However, it's completely abandoned!

In order to restore 100 Acre Wood, you must **read a book with yellow on the cover**! Once completed, the characters are restored and you are returned to the world outside the book.

Which location do you want to travel to next?

The Brolly Rail – turn to page 12.

Orion Found – turn to page 13.

9

T he trees have grown thick as you plunge into the Deepwoods. Noises surround you, mist befalls you, and a fabled creature springs from the shadows and attempts to attack you!

The only way to battle the foe is to **read a book that was published before 2000**! Yes! You've done it – you've slain the beast! Hurry along, or who knows what else will approach you in the Deepwoods?

Which location do you want to travel to next?

The Brolly Rail – turn to page 12.

Orion Found – turn to page 13.

Black Ice Bridge – turn to page 14.

Mermaids' Lagoon

L aughter and splashing can be heard from far off, so you follow the sounds hoping to find a friendly face. Turns out, you find *several* faces – but they're not friendly! The mermaids in Mermaids' Lagoon fear you and cocoon you with their song in the water.

You will be cocooned in their song until you **read a book featuring a female bond**! Once free, the mermaids realise they should not fear you and they allow you passage through Mermaids' Lagoon.

Which location do you want to travel to next?

Orion Found – turn to page 13.

Black Ice Bridge – turn to page 14.

11

The Brolly Rail

Buildings surround you, but you ignore them until you reach a chasm that can only be crossed using the brolly rail – except you don't have a brolly! At the nearby hotel, a young girl offers you hers, but she won't trade easily!

In order to gain the brolly, you must **read a book featuring transportation or has transportation on the cover**! Now you've done that, the magical girl gives you her brolly and wishes you luck. You step boldly towards the final location…

Are you ready for the final location?

The Book-Keeper's Stronghold – turn to page 15.

Orion Found

T he air is much warmer now as you stumble into a desert. The desert mountains seem to hide something – a spaceship that has crash landed! There is a crew of children stuck inside.

In order to free the children inside, you must **read a sci-fi book, or a book related to Space**! Once complete, you have the power to open the hatch and free the children. They thank you and help you traverse the rest of the desert until you reach the final location…

Are you ready for the final location?

The Book-Keeper's Stronghold – turn to page 15.

13

Black Ice Bridge

It's getting unbearably cold. Snow is falling and there's ice everywhere, making it dangerous to even move. You struggle, but you finally reach Black Ice Bridge.

In order to cross the bridge safely, you must **read a book featuring an expedition or adventure**! Once complete, you cast a spell that will allow you to cross Black Ice Bridge safely without slipping off. You try not to look down, but before you know it, your final location is before you…

Are you ready for the final location?

The Book-Keeper's Stronghold – turn to page 15.

ARE YOU SURE
YOU WISH TO PROCEED?
ARE YOUR INTENTIONS
FREE FROM GREED?
REMEMBER TO OBEY
THE QUESTER'S CREED.

NOW TAKE A STEP
INTO THE COLD
TO SAVE THE
BOOK-KEEPER'S
STRONGHOLD…

Huzzah! You're almost at your final destination! The Book-Keeper's Stronghold is near, but you need to cross a part of the snow sea to get there. You look around but for miles and miles, all you see is snow, and as you squint, you notice it is shifting!

Monsters! You were warned about these creatures. They're called Leviathans and they're TERRIFYING! You have nowhere to run as they approach. That is until you hear an approaching sleigh. The Leviathans change course and head for it. They circle round to pick you up, and a song-weaver on board manages to battle the monsters and protect you and the crew from a grisly fate.

The crew introduce themselves and you ask them to take you to the Book-Keeper's Stronghold. They agree to take you, and it isn't long before you reach the gates.

The entire place is protected by the witch, trapping everyone inside and keeping everyone out. You walk confidently to the gate, with all the knowledge and power you have gained from the stories you have read on your travels, and your moment has come.

In order to save the stronghold and defeat the witch, you must **read the next book in a series**! Once complete, you find yourself transported inside the stronghold now that you have been able to penetrate its defenses.

The witch, enraged, tries to banish you, but you're much too powerful now. With all the strength and courage you can muster, you finally defeat her. The curse has been lifted and the people of the Book-Keeper's Stronghold have been freed!

From outside, the stranger who sent you on the quest approaches you and thanks you greatly. He reveals himself – it's Gav of the Book-Keeper Stronghold! You have saved his stronghold, and in doing so, you have restored imagination in the Land of Make-Believathon.

THE END

The Prompts

The prompts for Believathon II are accompanied by locations in children's literature on the map. The goal of the locations is to celebrate and highlight the following children's books mentioned in this section.

This is a list of the prompts, the locations and the books that inspired them:

The Poacher's Pocket Inn is inspired by the location in *A Pinch of Magic* (2019) and *A Sprinkle of Sorcery* (2020) by Michelle Harrison. The prompt is to read the first book in a series. This can be any book that is considered the first in a series and can also be a book that has yet to have sequels released.

The Yellow Brick Road is inspired by the fictional road in *The Wonderful Wizard of Oz* (1900) by L. Frank Baum. The prompt is to read a book that you should have read years ago. This can be any book that has been on your TBR for a long time.

Baba Yaga's House is inspired by the version of the Russian folktale seen in Sophie Anderson's *The House With Chicken Legs* (2018). The prompt is to read a book featuring a family relationship. The family relationship can be a main theme or a background one, as long as there is some form of notable familial bond.

The Wonderfalls is a new location inspired by *Wonder* (2012) by R. J. Palacio. The prompt is to read a book featuring a disability. This can be a main character with a disability or a side character, as long as the character has some importance to the main story. You may also use a book that was written by an author with a disability.

100 Acre Wood is inspired by the setting featured in *Winnie-the-Pooh* (1926) by A. A. Milne. The prompt is to read a book with yellow on the cover. The yellow can be the whole cover, or just a part of the cover. The yellow can also be on the spine or back of the book, as long as there is some form of yellow on the book.

The Deepwoods is a location inspired by the Edge Chronicles series, specifically *Beyond the Deepwoods* (1998) by Paul Stewart and Chris Riddell. The prompt is to read a book that was published before the year 2000. As long as the book was published before, and not including, January 1st 2000, you can read it for this prompt.

Mermaids' Lagoon is inspired by the location in the play *Peter Pan* (1904), and novel *Peter and Wendy* (1911), by J. M. Barrie. The prompt is to read a book featuring a female bond. Any book that has two or more female characters with a prominent friendship, or are related, for example sisters, will work for this prompt.

The Brolly Rail is a magical transport system inspired by *Nevermoor* (2017) and *Wundersmith* (2018) by Jessica Townsend. The prompt is to read a book featuring transportation, or with transportation on the cover. This can be any form of transportation as long as it's rather prominent in the story. Alternatively, the book can have transportation on the cover.

Orion Found is a new location inspired by *Orion Lost* (2020) by Alastair Chisholm. The prompt is to read a sci-fi book, or a book related to Space. The book can have sci-fi elements to count, or as long as Space is part of the story. Alternatively, the book can have a Space-related word in the title to also count without being sci-fi or set in Space.

Black Ice Bridge is a location inspired by the *The Polar Bear Explorers' Club* series (2017-2019) by Alex Bell. The prompt is to read a book that features an expedition or an adventure. As long as the book has some form of travelling from one place to another for an important reason, it will count towards this prompt.

The Book-Keeper's Stronghold is a new location inspired by *Frostheart* (2019) and the upcoming *Frostheart 2: Escape from Aurora* (2020) by Jamie Littler. The prompt is to read the next book in a series. As long as the book is a continuation of a series, it will count. The book can also be a prequel as long as it was published after the original first book in the series.

The Book-Keeper's Stronghold idea was mainly inspired by the illustration Jamie Littler drew of host Gavin, which can be seen below:

Prompt Recommendations

If you find you are struggling to pick something for the prompts, help will always be given in the Land of Make-Believathon to those who ask for it. Here are a few people I consider expert readers in children's literature who have some suggestions on what to read:

Karen, Teacher & Book Blogger

Blog: kandobonkersaboutbooks.blogspot.com
Twitter: @karen_wallee

Poacher's Pocket
The first in a series

Who Let the Gods Out by Maz Evans
I love this series, mainly because it combines Greek Gods (a favourite at home when O was younger) & humour. I always say it's Percy Jackson meets David Walliams (but better written!). It also touches on some serious issues in a way children can understand.

Murder Most Unladylike by Robin Stevens

1940s boarding school, murders & 2 schoolgirls turned detectives. What's not to love? A brilliant series of books, with the final one due out later this year. Adventure & mystery that will keep you guessing. Agatha Christie for children.

City of Ghosts by Victoria Schwab
A ghost story that starts in America but quickly moves to Edinburgh. Adventure with tension & lots of creepiness thrown in. Currently 2 in the series but there's more on the way.

Tilly and the Bookwanderers by Anna James

I imagine that this series will be every book-lovers dream come true: living in a bookshop & being able to wander into books. Adventure amongst the pages of books is my idea of heaven.

Cogheart by Peter Bunzl
Victorian steampunk-style drama about a girl whose father goes missing. She & her best friend, as well as her mechanical fox, step-up to discover what's behind his disappearance. With hybrids, mechanicals & plenty of mystery set in Victorian London, you'll love these 4 books.

Yellow Brick Road
A book you should have read years ago

Swallows and Amazons by Arthur Ransome

Long summer days, children allowed to go off & camp on an island, meet with adventure & daring. I really wish I'd read this as a child!

When Hitler Stole Pink Rabbit by Judith Kerr | Another book I wish I'd read when I was a child. Based on Kerr's real-life escape from Germany at the start of WWII, the story gives a real insight into what life was like for Jewish families having to establish lives in new countries.

Mary Poppins by P. L. Travers
You've no doubt seen the film(s) which were wonderful but, by not reading the books, you'll be missing out on so much more that doesn't appear on screen (gingerbread wrapped in gilt paper stars; a funny night zoo where people are the main attraction …). Definitely worth a read.

Baba Yaga's House
A book featuring a family relationship

We Won an Island by Charlotte Lo
Since Luna's granny died, things have been different - Luna's dad has been depressed & the family have ended up owing too much rent on their flat & are forced to find somewhere else to live. Just in the nick of time, they win their very own Scottish island in a competition. I chuckled my way through this book & smiled a lot at the bond between Luna & her siblings, Margot & Fabien. This is a book that will make you want to head up to Scotland to dance on a beach!

Boy Underwater by Adam Baron
When 9-year-old Cymbelline has to be rescued during his first swimming lesson, his mum suffers a breakdown. Cymbelline vows to discover what secrets are being kept from him.

A wonderfully written book, full of emotion that bravely touches on adult mental health in a wonderful way.

24

The Girl Who Speaks Bear by Sophie Anderson | This book fizzles with magical beauty & there's a calmness to the writing that welcomes you in wraps you in a warm embrace. It's a perfectly woven mix of traditional tales & Yanka's story which, together, very much give the story a timeless quality. As the story unfolds, the excitement builds, leading towards a powerful message at the end of the book.

Mo, Lottie & the Junkers by Jennifer Killick
Mo's dad disappeared before he was born & now, 10 years on, he & his mum are moving in with his new stepdad & stepsisters, Lottie & Sadie. Their old house is just across the street from where they live now & Mo & Lottie quickly begin to realise that something very strange is now happening there. This is a fun & adventurous book with some crazy baddies!

 A Far Away Magic by Amy Wilson
Everything is different for Angel following the death of her parents: a new foster family & a new school to cope with; however, she is reluctant to make friends so why is she so drawn to Bavar? Could there be a link to the death of her parents? This is a captivating story that entwines magic & monsters.

The Wonderfalls
A book featuring a disability

Wonder by R. J. Palacio
This has to feature here & will be well-known for many things, including the quote 'when given the choice between being right or being kind, choose kind'. A heart-warming book which teachers us empathy & will make you want to hug the book.

What Katy Did by Susan Coolidge

One of my favourite books when I was a girl and, I think, a lesser-known Classic. Katy is a tomboy who resolves to be more like her invalid cousin Helen who is more compassionate. Her resolve lasts only a few hours … and then an accident means she is confined to her bedroom for a year and her life changes for ever. I recently reread this & still love it.

The Secret Garden by Frances Hodgson Burnett | Having lost her parents in a cholera epidemic in India, Mary returns to England alone, to the care of her Uncle Archibald whom she's never met. Life in his sprawling Yorkshire

home is lonely but then Mary finds the garden and Colin. A beautiful book.

Mermaids' Lagoon
A book featuring a female bond

Vote for Effie by Laura Wood

My class are currently loving this book about Effie who, having joined a new school (house move) is struggling to make friends, & the. Decides to run for student council against the most popular boy in school. An empowering read with laughs & a great style of writing.

A Pinch of Magic by Michelle Harrison

Join the Widdershins sisters in their magical journey when they discover that they're cursed, meaning they will die if they ever leave their town. I love all of Michelle Harrison's books, but

this is a real cracker (as is the follow-up, *A Sprinkle of Sorcery*).

The Afterwards by A. F. Harold

Ember & Ness are best friends, but when an accident at the park kills Ness, Ember feels lost & very alone … until she finds a way to get to the Afterworld, determined to bring her back. A heart-breaking story of female friendship with beautiful illustrations that add to the atmosphere, this book is guaranteed to make you cry … but it's completely worth it!

Not My Fault by Cath Howe

Maya and Rose are sisters. They are in the same class at school, but things haven't been great between the girls since the accident that badly damaged Maya's leg and they no longer talk to each other. Now they have a week-long school trip together to get through. This is a great story about sibling rivalry.

A Pocketful of Stars by Aisha Bushby

Looking at the strained relationship between a mum & her daughter following divorce, this is a book about family, friendships, growing-up & learning how to deal with the consequences of your actions. It's an emotionally & beautifully written novel that combines modern day gaming with traditional life in Kuwait.

100 Acre Wood

A book with yellow on the cover / spine / back

The Boy in the Tower by Polly Ho-Yen

Based on The Day of the Triffids, this is a great book by a brilliant author that I don't think always gets the recognition she deserves. A modern-day day plant apocalypse set in high-rise flats.

Can You See Me by Libby Scott & Rebecca Westcott | Tilly Adams is autistic and is terrified at the prospect of starting secondary school. She knows people don't understand her so she hides her autism as much as she can. This book is the story of one girl coping with high school and learning that it's ok to be yourself. This is a truly insightful book that should be in every classroom and read by every child and every adult. With diary extracts woven into the story, this is an honest and heart-felt novel that deserves a huge standing ovation.

And Then I Turned into a Mermaid by Laura Kirkpatrick | Funny & touching, this book looks at the everyday things young girls have to deal with (friendships, growing- up, families) but also how to keep the fact that you're a mermaid a secret ... more difficult than it looks when you need to stay away from water!

 Harry Potter and the Cursed Child by J. K. Rowling, John Tiffany & Jack Thorne
Why not slip a play script into your reading and find out what happens when Harry and Ginny's eldest heads to Hogwarts?

The Deepwoods
A book published before 2000

Northern Lights by Philip Pullman
After the success of the recent TV adaptation, why not find out how things started out with Lyra among the colleges of Oxford with her daemon and her Uncle Asriel. A classic novel that has to be read if you haven't already!

Holes by Louis Sachar
Stanley Yelnats is sent to a boys' detention center in America where he and the other boys are forced to dig holes every day. Stanley soon realises that there's more to the hole digging than first meets the eye and determines to discover exactly what the warden is up to. I read this book years ago and it's still one I recommend in school today.

Carrie's War by Nina Bawden

Evacuated during WWII, Albert, Carrie and Nick are billeted to Wales from London to live with Mr. Evans who is rather strict in his ways. They spend their time between there and the neighbouring farm where their lives will be changed forever. A wonderfully classic novel that I loved as a child and is still a firm favourite today.

Orion Found
A sci-fi book or related to Space

 ### The Infinite Lives of Maisie Day by Christopher Edge
| Maisie already has her GCSEs, A-levels & is studying for a degree in maths & physics. Today is her birthday ... her 10th birthday & all she wants is the equipment to build a nuclear reactor in her garage! The book tells us about Maisie's day seen from two alternate realities: one in which she wakes to find her parents downstairs & her dad making banana pancakes; the other where she wakes to find herself alone with a never-ending darkness outside her house which is slowly creeping her way. I'm really pleased that Christopher is making science cool and directed towards girls as well as boys.

Orion Lost by Alastair Chisholm

I couldn't not put this in here! It's been ages since we've had a great MG sci-fi book & this has all the components of a good sci-fi: space travel, hi-tech gadgets & alien life-forms, but I liked that the tech-talk didn't get over-complicated or dominate the plot; there was just enough to be realistic without the plot being lost to tech. It's an exciting & fast-paced story that will keep you on the edge of your seat, & there are several plot twists that will most definitely keep you guessing.

The Brolly Rail
A book featuring transport or on the cover

My Friend the Enemy by Dan Smith

I love all Dan Smith's books but this was the first one I read & so I have a soft spot for it! Set in Northumberland in 1941, Peter finds the German plane that was shot down over woods close to his home. When he goes to investigate, he finds a young German airman – the enemy. This is a compelling and exciting story that looks at war from a MG perspective.

Rumblestar by Abi Elphinstone

Casper accidentally finds himself in Rumblestar, one of the Unmapped Kingdoms, with Utterly Thankless, a girl who seems to be his complete opposite, things couldn't get much worse! However, Rumblestar is under threat from an evil harpy called Morg. A wonderful book full of quirky characters with brilliant names, Rumblestar is a story full of action & adventure which tells of friendship & being brave, even when you're scared. It shows us that heroes come in all shapes & sizes, & that being a hero can creep up on you quite unexpectedly.

Wildspark by Vashti Hardy

Beautifully written from the first page, this is a wonderfully exciting book with its own vivid world: a magical city with new ways of travelling & inventions to marvel at - I was drawn in from the beginning &, every time I put the book down, I felt part of me remained in Medlock. Wildspark is a story of family & friendship; of love & loss; of conquering your fears; of determination & hope. It's an exciting book with some truly unexpected twists - it's the perfect adventure!

Black Ice Bridge
A book featuring an expedition or an adventure

Boy 87 by Ele Fountain

Meet Shif: an ordinary boy who likes chess, maths & racing his best friend home from school. When soldiers come to his door, everything changes. Now he is forced to leave his family with only his best friend for company and embark on a very dangerous journey. Harrowing & heart-breaking in places, whilst heart-warming in others, this is a must-read book!

The Umbrella Mouse by Anna Fargher

Set in 1944, during WWII, Pip (a mouse) lives with her family inside an umbrella in a shop in Bloomsbury, when one night a bomb directly hits the shop, killing her entire family. Devastated and lost, Pip takes the umbrella (the first in England) and vows to take it to Gignesse in Italy, and so her adventures begin. Full of tension and with a host of heroes (none more-so than Pip), the book captures the war-time spirit and imparts many positive messages within its pages.

The Explorer by Katherine Rundell

Whilst on its way back to Manaus, a 6-seater plane crashes in the Amazon jungle, leaving the pilot dead & Fred, Con, Lila & Max, the four children on board, alone to fend for themselves. After several days, they decide they their only option is to find their own way out of the jungle. A wonderfully descriptive adventure during which the children stumble across some unexpected things.

The Eye of the North by Sinéad O'Hart

When Emmeline's parents (both scientists) go missing, she is sent to Paris aboard a ship; however, she soon discovers that the rather evil Dr. Bauer has other plans for her! He is desperate to get his hands on the mythical Kraken and he needs Emmeline in order to succeed. This is an action-packed adventure with a strong main character. You'll love it!

The Book-Keeper's Stronghold
The next book in a series

Choose the second book in any of the books in the Poacher's Pocket section. There are so many books I could recommend here – any of the What Katy Did books by Susan Coolidge, A Sprinkle of Sorcery by Michelle Harrison, and the sequels to Northern Lights by Philip Pullman!

– Karen
February 2020

Liam, Book Blogger

Blog: bookwormhole.co.uk
Twitter: @notsotweets

Poacher's Pocket
The first in a series

Poppy Pym and the Pharaoh's Curse by Laura Wood
The Bad Beginning by Lemony Snicket

The Yellow Brick Road
A book you should have read years ago

The Girl of Ink and Stars by Kiran Millwood Hargrave
Kensuke's Kingdom by Michael Morpurgo

Baba Yaga's House
A book featuring a family relationship

A Pinch of Magic by Michelle Harrison
Mo, Lottie and the Junkers by Jennifer Killick

The Wonderfalls
A book featuring a disability

Brightstorm by Vashti Hardy
The Christmasaurus by Tom Fletcher

Mermaids' Lagoon
A book featuring a female bond

The House of Hidden Wonders by Sharon Gosling
The Golden Butterfly by Sharon Gosling

100 Acre Wood
A book with yellow on the cover / spine / back

A Witch Alone by James Nicol

Holes by Louis Sacher

The Deepwoods
A book published before 2000

The Midnight Folk by John Masefield

The Worst Witch by Jill Murphy

The Brolly Rail
A book featuring transport or on the cover

First Class Murder by Robin Stevens

Wave Me Goodbye by Jacqueline Wilson

Orion Found
A sci-fi book or related to Space

The Starlight Watchmaker by Lauren James

Wildspark by Vashti Hardy

Black Ice Bridge
A book featuring an expedition or an adventure

The Eye of the North by Sinéad O'Hart

Skysong by Abi Elphinstone

The Book-Keeper's Stronghold
The next book in a series

Simply the Quest by Maz Evans

Alex Rider: Eagle Strike by Anthony Horowitz

– Liam, February 2020

Tsam, Bookseller and Blogger

Blog: aboywithabook.wordpress.com
Twitter: @tsamasaurusrex

Poacher's Pocket
The first in a series

Wolf Brother by Michelle Paver
I think *The Chronicles of Ancient Darkness* may have been my first book obsession, even more so than *Harry Potter*. I love the relationship between Torak and Wolf, this series has the perfect balance of magic, mystery, creepy bad guys, and an unbreakable friendship.

Nevermoor by Jessica Townsend

Imagine *Harry Potter*, but Hermione is the main character, and she isn't quite so cocky. That's *Nevermoor*. I adore Morrigan Crow and love her quest to find a family who don't believe she's cursed. Also, Fenestra, the Magnificat, is amazing and I want to be her friend.

The Yellow Brick Road
A book you should have read years ago

Anne of Green Gables by L.M. Montgomery
I definitely should have read this ages ago, I have it sitting on my shelf, but have never gotten round to it. Reading Tilly and the Bookwanderers, though, put it firmly back on my list and much further up.

Little Women by Louisa May Alcott
Given my love for books that make me cry (read: all books), you would've thought this would be one I'd sobbed over, but no. The recent film has made me want to read it even more, because I really need another book to cry over…

Baba Yaga's House
A book featuring a family relationship

Max Kowalski Didn't Mean It by Susan Day
I loved this book when I read it last year (for the first Believathon, one of the few I got through whilst getting married). A family mystery tied up with dragons and magic and finding yourself, it's an absolute must read.

Howl's Moving Castle by Diana Wynne Jones | Look, family isn't just the people you're related to. Your chosen family are the family you picked all for yourself. I can't think of a better story of a group coming together and forming a new, special family than Howl, Sophie, Calcifer and Michael.

The Wonderfalls
A book featuring a disability

Can You See Me? by Libby Scott & Rebecca Westcott | This is an amazing own-voices story about a girl with autism, and how people keep forgetting that she's there, or assuming she doesn't know what's happening. This book hits you like a sucker punch, but it's so very important.

Lenny's Book of Everything by Karen Foxlee

Just a heads up, this book will make you cry. It's beautiful, funny, a perfect description of a brotherly relationship, and it's also a reminder of exactly what's important in life, and how to make every moment count.

Mermaids' Lagoon
A book featuring a female bond

Tilly and the Bookwanderers by Anna James
This is a fairly new find for me, and I am hooked! Tilly is the kind of bookworm that should be familiar to us all, and her friendships with Anne (of Green Gables) and Alice (in Wonderland) are just perfect.

To Night Owl, From Dogfish by Holly Goldberg-Sloan & Meg Wollitzer

I love this book so much! Written entirely through a series of emails, it tells the story of two girls whose dads become a couple and force them to try and be friends. What ensues is just excellent.

100 Acre Wood
A book with yellow on the cover / spine / back

The Last Wild by Piers Torday
With all the suspense of a rickety bridge over a deep, dark chasm, coupled with some dark humour and an excellent series of chatty animal companions, this is a brilliant adventure story for everyone.

And Then I Turned into a Mermaid by Laura
Fitzpatrick | Imagine being a teenager and
working for your parents' fish and chip shop by
dressing as a haddock, and THEN finding out
you're also secretly a mermaid. Sounds crazy, and
kind of hilarious. Well, that's what this book is. I love that
it's filled with Laura's trademark sarcastic wit, and some
sisterly love that will warm the cockles of your heart
(seafood pun totally intended).

The Deepwoods
A book published before 2000

Redwall by Brian Jacques
Animals have power, in this medieval fantasy
world, that sees rats fighting mice, foxes
bartering with snakes, and all manner of forest
creatures caught up in a search for the Sword of
Martin the Great. A fantastic, magic-free adventure that I
loved as a kid.

The Demon Headmaster by Gillian Cross
I was terrified of the Demon Headmaster as a
child and, after having read it recently, he still
creeps me the heck out. Read this one if you're
willing to brave the shivers down your spine for
a brilliant story.

The Brolly Rail
A book featuring transport or on the cover

The Highland Falcon Thief by M. G.
Leonard & Sam Sedgman
I love a good train journey, and this was a
fantastic trip! Think Murder on the Orient
Express but with less killing and more dogs. An
A+ read, especially if you like a good mystery.

Brightstorm by Vashti Hardy

Flying ships, family drama, and a race to the South pole. Sounds like a good trip to me. The magical, fantastical skyships need to be real!

Orion Found
A sci-fi book or related to Space

Artemis Fowl by Eoin Colfer

One of my all-time favourite series ever, *Artemis Fowl* is the perfect blend of sci-fi (with a fleet of high-tech fairies and a computer nerd centaur) and fantasy ('cause they're fairies and centaurs… duh…) Everyone should read Artemis Fowl!

A Wrinkle in Time by Madeleine L'Engle

Another one that mixes magic and science, this journey through space and time to save a lost father has some slight 'Doctor Who' vibes and is totally fantastic.

Black Ice Bridge
A book featuring an expedition or an adventure

Around the World in Eighty Days by Jules Verne | OK, stay with me on this one. It's a full circuit around the world, there's an elephant, there's a bet for a HUGE amount of money, and there's a constant worry about someone having left a light on. The original adventure book, this is a must read!

The International Yeti Collective by Paul Mason | An expedition to find the yeti. An inquisitive young yeti who doesn't so much break the rules as demolishes them. I loved this snowy adventure and loved even more the friendship between Tick and Ella.

The Book-Keeper's Stronghold
The next book in a series

Mr. Penguin and the Catastrophic Cruise by Alex T. Smith | If you know me, you'll know that I'm a gigantic Mr. Penguin Fan, so I really, really need to read Book 3 and find out what the tentacles are all about!

The Christmasaurus and the Winter Witch by Tom Fletcher | It might be after Christmas now, but that doesn't mean I can't need some festiveness! I loved The Christmasaurus, so now I need to work out who this Winter Witch character is...

– Tsam
February 2020

Liam, Bookseller and Blogger

Blog: liamreads.co.uk
Twitter: @LiamOwens24

Poacher's Pocket
The first in a series

Who Let the Gods Out by Maz Evans
One of my new favourite books, WLTGO is a cross between Percy Jackson and Roald Dahl with one of the most exciting storylines I've ever come across in a Middle Grade book. Laugh-out-loud funny and incredibly heartfelt, readers are guaranteed to fall in love with the troublesome twosome that is Elliot and Virgo. I can't believe I didn't read this series sooner!

The Yellow Brick Road
A book you should have read years ago

Bridge to Terabithia by Katherine Paterson
I first read this book when I was 18 and I definitely wish I'd read it when I was younger. A wonderful story about friendship and the power of childhood imagination, *Bridge to Terabithia* is a beautiful story that explores grief and loss in a way that children can understand. A classic that everyone should read!

Baba Yaga's House
A book featuring a family relationship

Pax by Sara Pennypacker

Pets count as family, right? But do foxes count as pets? That's the problem Peter faces when he goes to live with his grandpa after his father goes to fight in the war. Forced to set his fox free into the wild, *Pax* is a story about the bond between humans and animals and the lengths you would go to to protect those you love. Told from the alternating viewpoints of Peter and Pax, Sara Pennypacker's novel is a brilliantly heartfelt story with all the charm and warmth of a Michael Morpurgo tale.

The Wonderfalls
A book featuring a disability

Wonder by R. J. Palacio

One of my top ten books of all-time, this is a one I recommend to adults as much as children. Never have I rooted for a character more than Auggie Pullman and I defy anyone not to fall in love with him after reading this book. Told from multiple perspectives, RJ Palacio shows how hard fitting in can be when you were born to stand out. A touching story about friendship, empathy and celebrating difference - it's easy to see why so many people have fallen in love with Wonder.

Mermaids' Lagoon
A book featuring a female bond

A Pinch of Magic by Michelle Harrison

I shouldn't really include this one in my recommendations because I know that Gav has already recommended this book to everyone, but I can't think of a stronger female bond than that shared between the Widdershins sisters in Michelle Harrison's spellbinding series. Forbidden magic, mysterious objects, and an ancient curse… it's simply too good to resist.

100 Acre Wood
A book with yellow on the cover / spine / back

Charlie Changes into a Chicken by Sam Copeland | Admittedly more gold than yellow but too fabulous a story not to recommend, *Charlie Changes into a Chicken* is a brilliant book towards the younger end of the Middle Grade bracket and ideal for reluctant readers. Funny and moving in equal measure, Sam Copeland's debut explores stress and anxiety in a way that's accessible for kids. Oh, and he talks about poo. Like, all the time. What's not to love?

The Deepwoods
A book published before 2000

 Say Cheese and Die by R. L. Stine
One of my favourite childhood memories is staying over my grandparents' house and staying up late reading *Goosebumps* in bed in the dark with a torch. The one I remember best though is this one … a chilling story about a group of kids who explore an abandoned mansion and uncover a cursed camera that predicts terrifying visions of the future! To this day, it's one of my favourite children's horror stories.

The Brolly Rail
A book featuring transport or on the cover

Potkin and Stubbs by Sophie Green
This does feature a monorail on the cover so that'll do for me. A wonderful paranormal mystery with a noir vibe, *Potkin and Stubbs* has quickly become one of my favourite Middle Grade books and I love recommending it to others. It's filled with twists and turns and a whole cast of brilliant characters. Go give it a try - I guarantee you'll not regret it!

Orion Found
A sci-fi book or related to Space

The Kid Who Came From Space by Ross Welford | From one of the best talents in children's books, *The Kid Who Came From Space* follows Ethan as he tries to track down his twin sister Tammy who mysteriously vanished on Christmas Eve. Featuring hairy, smelly aliens, a talking spaceship and a pet chicken called Suzy, this is quite possibly my favourite Ross Welford book yet!

Black Ice Bridge
A book featuring an expedition or an adventure

The Polar Bear Explorers' Club by Alex Bell Stella wants to be an explorer like her father. There's just one problem… according to The Polar Bear Explorers' Club, girls can't be explorers. So when Stella sets out on an expedition of her own, she's determined to prove them all wrong. A spellbinding blustery adventure story of survival and friendship, this is the sort of book you'll devour in a single sitting!!

The Book-Keeper's Stronghold
The next book in a series

A Sprinkle of Sorcery by Michelle Harrison, or *Potkin and Stubbs: The Haunting of Peligan City* by Sophie Green. My TBR list is a mile long so I haven't made it to these sequels quite yet but I'm confident they'll be just as good as their predecessors… if not better!

– Liam
February 2020

The Magic of Middle Grade

On the Believathon twitter, I asked what middle grade has meant to you and if Believathon has helped you with your passion for middle grade. This is the incredible response from **you**, the community! I wanted **you** to be part of this compendium the most.

@MeAsIShouldBeB1
Believathon gave me the opportunity to reread some of my favourite MG books. Ones that I hadn't picked up in years and some that I read every year. It got me to finally reread Harry Potter. Not only that, it got me through a really bad time. I am so thankful for Believathon.

@Colleen_Quinn
I was so excited for a MG readathon since I am a MG teacher! My students loved completing it too. Last year during Believathon my students read more than 30 books! It was the first time many of them completed a readathon and now they're hooked!

@faeryartemis
Middle grade lifted me out of a dark place, they aren't just for children they are full of hope & empathy for a better, happier, kinder world, even when dealing with the toughest

of topics. Reading Middle Grade as an adult puts me in the 'Age of Believing again' after years adrift. Believathon was a fun way to give me added incentive to read slightly less new MG books on my shelves that fitted the prompts to giving love to those books not so in the spotlight anymore. Which I am so very grateful for!

@Ravenous_Reads
Some of my favorite books of all time are MG but still I don't tend to pick them up. Believathon showed me my love for children's books again and I now try to consciously read at least one a month. Thank you for bringing this joy back into my life!

@daydreamwishes7
Believathon for me was phenomenal and brought my lust for books back to life and middle grade brought back the magic I thought that I had long lost. I read some of the most amazing books and found my best read of the year. Without Believathon I wouldn't have got that.

@Teri_readsbooks
Like most people here, I started reading at a young age and fell in love with everything about books, then life happened. I grew up and the next thing I know I'm married with a full-time job and reading has fallen to the wayside. I am now 50 and was diagnosed with MS in August of this year. I became depressed and went to a very dark place. My husband suggested I start reading to occupy my mind. I picked up a few books and could not get into them…. then I saw Believathon. I got excited when I saw the prompt to re-read a childhood favorite. I challenged myself to complete all the challenges. While reading the middle grade books I could almost feel a weight lifting. *Frostheart* and *The Way Past Winter* in particular encouraged me to face my life challenges head on the same way the characters in these books did. I felt encouraged and I also rediscovered the joy books could

bring in the same way I did when I first started reading! Thank you so much for all the effort you put into the readathon and all the encouragement you gave along the way.

@trace16
Middle grade books are so important to me as they cover so many different genres from fantasy to adventure to hard-hitting contemporary books, and each book always teaches some important lessons that we all could learn. For me, I was able to escape my normal life.

@Stephloves4
MG has become a huge part of my reading experience. I always read *Winnie The Pooh* repeatedly but until I came across your channel Gavin, I'd never really opened my mind to MG properly. Believathon reinforced that, and I have the most fun when reading MG now. Thank you.

@NeverlandIngrid
I've always loved MG. I read mostly to escape, and MG is perfect for that. The language is easier (English isn't my first language) so getting immersed in the story is easier. Therefore, they're also quicker to read than older books and make me stay out of book slumps. I also think they add a unique perspective to stories. To see the world through children's eyes is magic in itself. What I loved about Believathon was that I got so many great recommendations. I discovered your channel not long before. I had struggled with finding recommendations for middle grade before that. And now I have so many! I feel like Believathon helped "normalize" (not sure if it's the right word) adults reading middle grade. At least in the corner of booktube I hang out in. Which is amazing. Lastly, I got to connect to other middle grade readers. Oh, and I got to discover new amazing authors and have some cool interactions with them!

@catsandteabooks

Believathon reminded me of the magic of middle grade and has led to me going to that part of bookstores much more often! I love how hopeful the stories often are and the optimism of the characters.

@Confuzzledom

I always read children's books but usually interspersed with others. It was so fun to have a whole month of it. Last year wasn't the best for me and Believathon gave me a chance to escape back to my childhood. Even when the books had real-life issues, they weren't adult issues, so it felt like I was getting away from it all without even leaving my couch.

@books4wendy

I'm so glad you started Believathon! I love middle grade books. They are so much fun, and it is nice to see other people reading them without the hang-up of "you're too old to read that". We should be able to read what makes us happy and middle grade books do that for me.

@ThatsMyBook

Believathon helped me focus on my reading again and break my reading block - which many adults have, especially now we've found the free time to be on our phones for everything except reading fiction! I read more kids books for myself now, not just for my daughter.

@notsotweets

Believathon got me picking those books off my shelves that I'd been neglecting for too long. My favourite thing about reading middle grade is that I can share my excitement with my kids.

@_NeverendingTBR

I never really read middle-grade until the Believathon and

it's helping get my stepson into reading more for pleasure rather than just for school.

@Mummy2aRockStar

I love middle grade as some of the books are so full of magic and adventure without the boundaries that are sometimes set in adult books that you can get lost in an entirely new world and I love sharing that with my son. I only wish others were as like-minded as the Believathon following when it comes to there being no age limit as I have been shamed for picking a children's book from the library.

@aerialflight

2019 was the year I got back into reading, and quite a few of them were middle grade books! I ended up falling in love with MG books and discovered just how much it had to offer to the world. The Believathon has sparked my excitement to expand my horizons!

@Applebrush1

I have read the replies left so far. Honestly, I can't come close to the power behind some of these stories, nor do I even want to try. I do want to participate this time. I love to read, and for the longest time, it would only be children's books. Never understood why they would divide books into groups and sub-groups. But even as a teenager, I preferred children's books because I thought the older stuff was romances and I would rather ram my eyes out with a rusty fork than read anything romantic. Now I read just about anything but romances and westerns, but whenever I pick something to read just because, it would be a children's classic. Or Mercedes Lackey, who I think writes children books in disguise.

@RozyRavenclaw

Believathon opened a whole new world of books to me. I never thought to look into the genre until Believathon and now it is one of my go-tos. I have found some all-time favorites since Believathon and feel at home in these books. Middle grade is awesome for all ages!

@RigsPeltLove
I loved doing Believathon last year and it's made me love reading middle grade. A lot of the time I prefer them to adult books.

@HannahJM1806
Since finding MG last year, it has been my saviour at times when I've needed to escape. Believathon was the first readathon I'd ever done, it helped me focus my reading dependent on the prompts and fall in love with all genres of MG and read ones that were out of my comfort zone.

@IamPoodles
At times I can barely switch off from work, let alone read. Believathon forced me (willingly) to pick up some new MG and they were honestly like therapy. When I'm feeling anxious, they are my go-to now and that's solely because of Believathon introducing me to so many amazing books.

@fragrantpages
I'm so sad I missed it last time, I remember thinking "MG isn't really for me" but after watching both you and Alexandra Roselyn, I have come to realize how AMAZING middle grade is and now I'm inspired to write my own! I'm so excited to participate this time. MG is the best!

@SophiaZarifis
It's really nice sometimes to read a book that does not have any sex, violence or profanities in it. Just a good story.

@Valda_Varadinek
So many fabulous MG books have been/being released into the wild. I love the idea of Believathon & Believathon 2 to

raise the profile of reading particularly for MG readers.

@llykaios
Believathon was the readathon I'd always wanted! I sorely regret I was too busy to make a video about it, but I thoroughly enjoyed it!!

@Nurse_who_reads
MG brought me back to my childhood when I loved reading. It feels me with joy and happiness to read MG.

@laureads_
Seeing this readathon on your own channel helped me become interested in middle grade and now I'm obsessed. I love it!

@darthvixreads
I had been having a tough, stressful time when I decided to participate in Believathon, and it was just what I needed. It brought magic and wonder to stressful days and inspired me to read at least one middle grade per month in 2020. I am at 3 for 2020 & looking forward to more.

@homeinabook
Since the new year I have been re-reading and re-falling in love with the Roald Dahl books and as of yesterday started my epic re-reading of the Harry Potter series. A good book doesn't have a cut off age.

@mum_of_feral5
I've just discovered Believathon and haven't investigated fully yet. I work in KS2 and use novels as a way to connect with pupils. I read as many as I can get my hands on and use this to engage with the kids and find common ground with them. I'm a TA, I like to think making these connections with the kids gives us a bond that they'll respond to and if even just one of them makes a good decision because of it,

that makes it worthwhile.

@drinkreadblog
I've been a life-long reader, but middle grade and chapter books are some of the stories that still stick with me today. A-Z Mysteries, Magic Tree House, Harry Potter, Percy Jackson, the Storm Runner series, are just some of the stories that have shaped my love for reading.

@AngiBelle1
I rarely read books that aren't middle grade... I've just never been able to get into fiction written for adults!

A huge thank you to everyone who participated in the first Believathon in November 2019 and had the nicest things to say about their experience with it. It means the world to me to know that my little readathon helped somewhat when it comes to picking up middle grade books. They can be a light in the darkness for so many people, and I know how important they can be for shaping so many people from an early age. To absolutely everyone – thank you, thank you, thank you!

– Gavin

Remember to follow
@Believathon
on Twitter and Instagram
for regular news, updates
and giveaways.

"Happiness can be found,
even in the darkest of times,
if one only remembers
to turn on the light."
– J. K. Rowling

Printed in Poland
by Amazon Fulfillment
Poland Sp. z o.o., Wrocław